Troto

and the TRUCKS

Uri Shulevitz

Margaret Ferguson Books

FARRAR STRAUS GIROUX

New York

Farrar Straus Giroux Books for Young Readers
175 Fifth Avenue, New York 10010

Copyright © 2015 by Uri Shulevitz
All rights reserved
Color separations by Bright Arts (H.K.) Ltd.
Printed in the United States of America
by Phoenix Color, Hagerstown, Maryland
First edition, 2015
10 9 8 7 6 5 4 3 2 1

mackids.com

Library of Congress Cataloging-in-Publication Data
Shulevitz, Uri, 1935– author, illustrator.
    Troto and the trucks / Uri Shulevitz. — First edition.
        pages cm
    Summary: Troto is a happy little car who likes to go places until he drives all the way to
Cactusville and meets some big trucks that tease him for being so small.
    ISBN 978-0-374-30080-7 (hardback)
    [1. Automobiles—Fiction.   2. Trucks—Fiction.   3. Teasing—Fiction.   4. Size—Fiction.
5. Automobile racing—Fiction.]   I. Title.

PZ7.S5594Tro 2015
[E]—dc23
                                                        2014040549

Farrar Straus Giroux Books for Young Readers may be purchased for business or promotional use.
For information on bulk purchases please contact Macmillan Corporate and Premium Sales
Department at (800) 221-7945 x5442 or by email at specialmarkets@macmillan.com.

For Margaret Ferguson and Angus Killick

Troto was a happy little car

who liked to go places.

One day after a long drive,

he came to a town called Cactusville.

When the trucks saw Troto, they burst out laughing.

"Hey, guys, what's that little thing?" asked Big Red.

"It's a bug on wheels," said Big Blue.

"Careful, don't step on it," said Big Yellow.

They couldn't stop laughing.

Troto didn't feel so happy anymore. He didn't like being laughed at.
I'll show them what a little one can do, he thought.

"Hey, big guys," he said, "want to race me? Meet me at Cactus Canyon at high noon."

The trucks were very excited. They couldn't wait to get started.

When high noon came, the race began.

The trucks took off,

leaving Troto in the dust.

But then Big Red got a flat tire.

I can jump over, thought Troto.

Big Blue almost flipped.

I can scoot around, thought Troto.

Big Yellow got stuck.

I can squeeze through, thought Troto.

I might win this race!

And he did.

The trucks were no longer laughing. "You may be little, but you sure are quite a car," they said. "Congratulations!"

"Thanks," said little Troto . . .

. . . and he drove off into the sunset, casting a big shadow.